Dear Fellow Story Explorers,

Thank you for picking up this extraordinary book!
You are holding a unique text, the culmination
of many helping hands and one remarkable young
author. A young author who participated in an exciting
and interactive writing program called Share Your Story!
Share Your Story is a nationally acclaimed writing
program which mentors aspiring authors through
an eight-step writing process. Opportunities to interact
virtually with published authors are provided so that
participants gain insight and feedback about their new craft!
This program addresses barriers that may prevent students
from participating in meaningful literacy experiences.

Leap for Literacy offers several initiatives, including Read-N-Roll,
which uses kindness as the currency for students to build their
personal collection of books, the Read-It-Forward-athon which
is a fundraiser fueled by minutes read and acts of kindnes,
and the Leap For Literacy Publishing Program. This program
allows students from the Share Your Story Program the
opportunity to submit their books for consideration
to be published and professionally illustrated!

You are holding a true labor of love! Please share this
powerful book with another Story Explorer and support
our mission to create meaningful literacy opportunities
for students in our community and across our country.

Yours in Learning,

Stanley T Tucker

Stanley T. Tucker
Founder, Leap for Literacy
Host of The Very Airy Library

Go to www.leapforliteracy.org to learn about
all our programs & how you can get involved!

MW00977023

LEAP *for* LITERACY

THE VERY AIRY LIBRARY
WITH STAN TUCKER

SHARE YOUR STORY

read 'n roll

ISBN: 978-1-956328-17-2

GRAYSON'S MISSION to MARS

by Grayson Albers

This book
belongs to:

_____

This book
is dedicated to
my family.

TODAY

is going to be the

biggest

day
of my life

because...

Now I'm heading to the Launch pad.

So, I get my suit on and I hop on the rocket.

Fun Fact Box:
I'm Grayson from Dallas,
Georgia, and I'm ten years old!

5... 4...

3...

2... 1...

Finally, after a looong journey we made it to Mars.

Now to begin my mission...
to find and fix Perseverance.

So I searched...

And searched...

Now to fix its arm because samples are breaking.

So I grab a tray and put it on the arm.

Now it can grab samples!

Now it's time to go home....

THE
END.

A PEEK AT THE ORIGINAL BOOK FROM THE AUTHOR

On these pages you can see some of Grayson's original ideas!

Grayson has a goal, a dream, and we are so happy he wrote this story about it.

TODAY
is going to be the
biggest
day
of my life
because...

TODAY is going to be the

Biggest day of My life

Because...

5... 4...
3...
2... 1...

We like to show the author's original drawings to show how the illustrator's art is inspired.

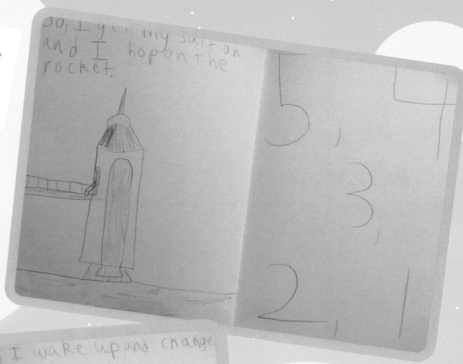

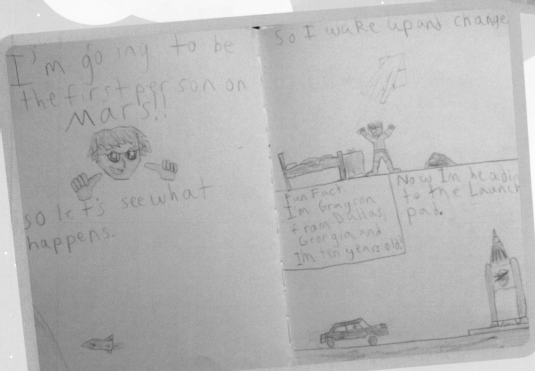

Grayson, you did a great job!

Interesting Facts about Mars:

Mars is first discovered by early astronomers using telescopes in 1600's.

(Source: MARS IS by Suzanne Slade)

Mars has 2 very small moons named Deimos and Phobos. They are shaped like potatoes.

(Source: National Geographic Kids: Little Kids First Big Book of Space by Catherine D. Hughes)

A day on Mars is just half an hour longer than a day on Earth. However, Mars moves around the sun at a slower speed than Earth, which means a year lasts much longer. One year on mars is 687 Earth days!

(Source: Mars: Explore the mysteries of the Red Planet by Smithsonian)

The rover SOUJOURNER was the first vehicle with wheels used to explore another planet.

(Source: National Geographic Kids: Little Kids First Big Book of Space by Catherine D. Hughes)

Mars is about half the size of Earth, and it has some of the most spectacular scenery in the solar system.

(Source: National Geographic Kids: SPACE Encyclopedia, Written & Illustrated by David A. Aguilar)

Mars has the largest volcano in the solar system called Olympus Mons.

(Source: Space A Visual Encyclopedia by Smithsonian)

More Interesting Facts about Mars to Explore Online:

National Geographic Kids:
https://www.natgeokids.com/uk/discover/science/space/facts-about-mars/

Ducksters:
https://www.ducksters.com/science/mars.php

NASA Science Space Place:
https://spaceplace.nasa.gov/all-about-mars/en/

Little House of Science:
https://www.littlehouseofscience.com/20_fascinating___fun_science_facts_planet_mars

Planets for Kids:
https://www.planetsforkids.org/planet-mars.html

Grayson Albers Bio:

Grayson is currently a 5th grader from Dallas, GA where he's a huge help taking care of the family's farm – potbelly pig, goats, and chickens.

He loves to read, draw, build Lego's and horseback ride. He's currently an Arrow of Light in scouts and cannot wait to become an astronaut as he aspires to go to space and be the first person to Mars! He hopes you enjoy his book.

To learn about when the the next Share Your Story program is,
go to www.leapforliteracy.org
so you too can become a published author like Grayson!

Made in the USA
Columbia, SC
29 October 2023